I0607275

THE SCHOOLDAYS OF JACK AT ETON

EDWIN J. BRETT, Limited, HARKAWAY HOUSE, 6, WEST HARDING STREET, LONDON, E.C.
And all Booksellers.

JACK AT ETON;

or,

The Adventures of Two College Chums.

By a Popular Author.

BEAUTIFULLY ILLUSTRATED.

COMPLETE.

LONDON:

HARKAWAY HOUSE, 6, WEST HARDING STREET, FETTER LANE,
FLEET STREET, E.C., AND ALL BOOKSELLERS.

The Schooldays of Jack at Eton.

"THE EVIL-LOOKING TIMOR GAVE THE CAGE A KICK."

No. 1.

PRICE ONE HALFPENNY.

[PUBLISHED EVERY MONDAY.]

With this Number is Presented gratis a Splendid Coloured Picture.

THE SCHOOLDAYS OF JACK AT ETON;

OR,

The Adventures of Two College Chums.

CHAPTER I.

THE CHUMS MEET.

"THE First and Second Forms, and the Lower School, will return to Eton on the 14th of April. The Fourth Form and Removes and the Upper School on the 15th. The Sixth Form on the 16th."

Such was the announcement in the newspapers, and as may be imagined, quite a number of boys assembled at the Great Western station in London on the fourteenth.

The station in the afternoon was crowded by Etonians, who were anxious to catch the half-past three train from Paddington, and get down before dark to college.

This is not to be wondered at, when it is considered that Eton contains nearly a thousand boys, has nearly 20 masters, including classical and mathematical masters, the boys living in different houses, dotted about the college precincts, and going at certain hours to the school buildings, which are in a central position on the Slough Road.

Among the boys who were looking after their luggage on the platform was one who appeared to take a great interest in a canary bird in a gilded cage.

He was tall, fair, and not bad-looking, about fourteen years of age, but too slim to be very strong.

"Put that bird in the carriage with me, porter," said he, pointing to a first-class in which he had placed some books and papers.

"Yes, sir. One moment, sir," replied the porter, who was busily engaged in waiting on another young gentleman.

He was expecting a tip, for he knew that Eton boys are always generous in return for any little attention paid them.

The boy turned his back for a while, and a stout, thick-set, dark-complexioned young fellow stumbled up against the cage, upsetting it.

"Halloa!!" cried the owner of the bird, who heard it fall, and instantly turned round; "what did you do that for?"

"Because I couldn't help it," was the reply.

"I believe you did it on purpose."

"You have a perfect right to your own opinion," said the other boy, who spoke with a strong foreign accent.

He had not the look of an Englishman, but seemed to spring from a different race.

Rings sparkled on his fingers, a diamond pin flashed in his scarf, he wore a heavy gold watch chain with two lockets, and was evidently well off.

"Pick it up again," cried the boy with the bird.

"I'll see you hanged first, and then I won't," was the reply.

"Who are you?"

"My name's Timor. I've no reason to be ashamed of it. If you want me, I'm an Eton boy, and you'll hear of me in the college."

"My name's Owen Tudor," exclaimed the other, who was red with rage. "I'm a Welshman, and in my country we don't stand any nonsense."

"I'm a Russian. My father's attached to the embassy here," said Timor, "and if I had you in Russia, I'd have you knouted till you learnt how to keep a civil tongue in your head."

"Well, I must say you look like the villain of old, Timon the Tartar," laughed Owen Tudor.

"Yes, you will find me a Tartar if

you provoke me, so I advise you to be more civil to me in future."

"Pick up my birdcage," cried the Welsh boy.

"I shan't, and that's as flat as the valley of the Volga."

Owen Tudor did not want to make a scene at the railway station.

But, at the same time, he did not care about putting up with the young Russian's insolence.

He advanced to him with a threatening gesture.

"Oh!" exclaimed Timor, "your bird seems to be a great worry to you. I think I will relieve you from it."

"What do you mean?"

"Simply this."

The evil-looking Timor gave the cage a kick with his foot, which opened the door, and the bird being liberated from its confinement, flew up to the roof of the station, where it perched on a rafter among some very smutty sparrows, who all began to chirp at his intrusion, some of the more indignant pecking at him.

This was more than Owen Tudor could stand.

"Confound you, take that!" he said, aiming a blow at him.

Timor warded it off with a cane he carried in his hand, and the whistle blowing for the train to start, he jumped into a carriage, the guard locking the door.

He gave the guard half-a-sovereign in an ostentatious manner.

"Keep this carriage for me," he said; "I want it to myself. I hate travelling with a lot of cads."

Owen Tudor was furious.

Shaking his fist at the aristocratic young Russian, who was laughing impudently at him, he exclaimed—

"Come out of that and fight me like a man."

"I can't," replied Timor.

"Why not?"

"For two reasons."

"What are they?"

"In the first place, I don't want to kill you at present; secondly, I'm locked in."

The guard touched Owen Tudor on the shoulder.

"Now, sir, if you're going on," he said.

He held open the door of a carriage, and as the train was already beginning to move, Owen bestowed one malignant glance at Timor and another sad one at the empty cage.

Then he stepped in, the door was shut, and the train rolled out of the station.

He found himself in the company of two boys, one of whom sat opposite him, and was stout, well-built, healthy, and apparently good-tempered, with a profusion of curly hair, clear blue eyes, and a well-cut mouth.

The other was small, rather undersized, decidedly ugly, with a comical expression of countenance, and a sort of perpetual grin on his face.

"I say," exclaimed the one opposite Owen, "excuse me for talking to you, but that was a beastly shame of that big fellow. I saw him kick the cage over, and if it had come to a row I'd have helped you."

"Would you?"

"Yes, I would, for he is too much for one of your age. You said your name was Tudor, didn't you? Mine is Jack Dashley."

"Thanks for your sympathy," replied Owen. "I think I could have got at the great big brute if the train hadn't started so soon."

"He's a regular Russian Bear, and looks as strong," said Jack Dashley.

"Russian Bear, yes, that's the only name for him," answered Owen. "I liked that bird. It was a parting present from my mother."

"Are you a new fellow?" asked Jack Dashley.

"Yes. Are you?"

"I am. My people wanted to see me off, but I chose to come alone. We have been down to Eton, and I know where I am going, so I didn't want any kissing and hand-shaking at the station; it is bad form."

"Just my case," said Owen. "Have you ever been to school before?"

"Oh, yes. I was three years at a private school. This is my first shy at a public one," answered Dashley.

"I had a private tutor at home. Whose house are you going to at Eton?"

"Mr. Dryasdust's," replied Jack Dashley. "And you?"

"By Jove! that is strange. He is to be my master too. I say, we ought to chum up, you and I."

"We will. I'm agreeable," said Jack Dashley. "I like your looks."

"So do I yours. Is it a bargain, old fellow?" cried Owen.

"It is, as far as I am concerned. We will be chums all the time we are at college, and make an alliance, offensive and defensive against the Russian Bear."

"Agreed."

They shook hands cordially, and the compact was sealed.

The third boy in the carriage could not help hearing what they were talking about, and when they had finished he spoke.

"Excuse me, you two new fellows, he exclaimed. "I am an old boy in my second half at Eton, and I can tell you a great deal about the school."

"I suppose you can," replied Jack Dashley.

"Let me introduce myself."

"I shall be very glad to know you."

Owen Tudor echoed this sentiment, and with the true instinct of Eton boys, they bowed to one another like little men.

"My name's Jimmy Jingo," continued the third boy, "and I board at Butler's. That's the next house to yours in Keat's Lane."

"Who's Keat?" asked Jack.

"He was head master once upon a time. Why he had a lane I don't know, but that's what they call it. He was the flogging head master, and would birch a fellow for being two minutes' late for school."

"That's pleasant," remarked Owen Tudor.

"You wouldn't say so if you were in for it."

"Are there a nice set of fellows at our house?" asked Jack.

"Not particularly. They bully a good deal, and you'll find the fagging rather hard."

"Do you know Timor?"

"Don't I? and I hate him. We had a fight once, and he licked me in no time. I'd like to see some one tackle him. He's in your house, and you'll have all you want of him. They say his father is awfully rich in Russia, and his mother is a lady of English rank; but he's more Russian than English."

"So I should think."

"They tell funny tales about him at your tutor's," continued Jimmy Jingo. "I've heard that he keeps a cane in his room to thrash the small boys."

During the remainder of the journey Jimmy Jingo gave them much valuable information, which it is unnecessary to repeat here, and by the time they reached their destination they knew so much about Eton that they fancied they had been there six months.

Arriving at Windsor, Jack Dashley and Owen Tudor took a cab, and were driven across the river Thames into the village of Eton.

Then they crossed the bridge over Barn's Pool, and were in the sacred precincts of the college.

Jack was the son of a fashionable doctor in London, who was personally known to Mr. Dryasdust.

Owen sprang from an old Welsh family, and his father and grandfather had been educated at Eton.

Mr. Dryasdust received the boys kindly, and showed them to their rooms, which were plainly furnished, each having a table, a shut-up bedstead—let down at night—three chairs, and a carpet.

Everybody has his own room, in which he takes his breakfast and tea.

He was allowed a pound of sugar and a quarter-of-a-pound of tea every week.

A slice of bread and a pat of butter was supplied at each meal.

Anything else he wanted he had to buy.

Dinner and supper were served in the dining room, when all sat down together.

There were two galleries in the house, one above the other, each containing about twenty rooms, so that there were forty boys in the house when full.

An old woman waited upon the inmates of each gallery, and the name of the one on Jack's floor was Susan.

Jack found that his room adjoined that of Owen's.

A nice fire burned in the grate, and Susan had laid the cloth as the boys entered, while the small tea kettle hissed merrily.

You two young gents seem to be friends," she remarked; "and I should advise you to mess together."

"We met for the first time to-day," replied Jack. "But we have arranged to be chums all the time we are at college. What do you mean by messing together?"

"Taking your meals, sir?"

"Oh, I see—a very good idea. What do you say, Owen?"

Owen Tudor was quite pleased, and a servant just then brought up a little hamper of good things, with which Mrs. Dashley had provided her son.

A couple of fowls, a ham, sundry pots of jam, and a boiled tongue are rather calculated to quicken the appetites of two hungry boys.

"You makes your own tea, sir," exclaimed Susan. "It's lock-up at six at this time of the year, supper at nine, prayers at half-past, and candles taken away at ten. I'll call you in the morning at seven, in time for school."

Mr. Dryasdust had previously tested the capacity of the boys, and had informed them that they would be placed in the fourth form, the lowest division of the upper school.

Sitting down to tea, they felt quite at home, and began to enjoy themselves.

"This isn't half bad," observed Jack, with his mouth full of ham and fowl."

"None so dusty," replied Owen. "I've fared worse."

While he spoke the door opened, and a dark-haired boy, with a sneaking look, entered.

"Who are you?" asked Jack, looking up; "and what do you want?"

"I'm Funnybird Minor," was the reply.

"Minor! what does that mean?"

"What a fool you are not to know that. Minor means less, and major great. I've got a big brother. He's Funnybird Major, and I'm called Funnybird Minor, to distinguish us."

"You look like a funny bird. You're all legs and wings, and you've got a beak like a pelican," said Jack.

Funnybird Minor certainly had a very big nose, curved somewhat like a beak, but he did not like this allusion to it.

"Don't you chaff my nose," he said. If my major heard you, there'd be a row, and you'd be in it."

"Really?"

"Yes, really. You can sneer, but my major always licks fellows who cheek me. I did not come here to have a row, though. You smelt so good from the outside, that I thought I'd come and see what you had got to eat."

"Your nose guided you."

Let my nose alone, I tell you, it don't belong to you," cried Funnybird Minor.

"I should be sorry if it did, but I'm not touching it—wouldn't touch it with a pair of tongs," replied Jack.

Funnybird eyed the tongue in a hungry way.

"Give us some of that. I did'nt bring any grub back with me," he said.

"That's no reason why you should come cadging from us," replied Owen Tudor.

"Won't you let me join you?"

"No," said Jack and Owen in a breath.

"Then I'll tell my brother; he'll soon make you," threatened Funnybird Minor. "My major likes me. He's second cock of the house; only Careless the captain can lick him, and he messes with Timor. What Timor and he can't do is'nt worth doing."

"You little beast, get out," cried Owen, "or, as I'm a Welshman, I'll put you out."

"A Welshman," are you?"

"Yes, I am, and there's nothing to be ashamed of in that."

"Ba-a-a! you look like a Welsh goat! ba-a-a!" cried Funnybird Minor, retreating to the door.

Jack Dashley threw a piece of bread at him, which he narrowly dodged by ducking his head.

"Wait till I tell my major," he said. "Ba-a-a!"

Then he disappeared through the door.

"He's a cool fish," remarked Jack, "I wonder if there are many more like him in the house?"

"Hang his impudence," said Owen, whose face was flushed. "He 'ba-a-ed' at me like a goat, and I can't stand that."

Jack was afraid there was trouble brewing, because Funnybird Minor had a vindictive, bad face, and if his brother was as strong as he said, it was no use resisting him, for a small boy cannot fight one older and stronger than himself.

Then again, he was a friend of Timor's.

They messed together, and it would be absurd for either himself or Owen to tackle the Russian, who was too big for them.

That fellow Funnybird is a hot member," remarked Jack, "and I'm a false prophet if there is not going to be a row."

"I think so too," answered Owen; "let's hide the grub."

"Good!" I'll do it," said Jack.

He hurriedly removed the things from the table and put them on the top of the shut-up bedstead, which was the only hiding-place he could think of, and that was not a very secure one, yet it was better than none.

Scarcely had he succeeded in doing so, and resumed his place at the table, than the door opened.

A tall, thick-set boy, who was Funnybird Major, and the evil-looking Timor entered, while young Funnybird stood behind them.

CHAPTER II.

THE FIRST NIGHT AT ETON.

"What's your name, you new fellow?" cried Funnybird.

Jack told him, as did Owen on being asked a similar question.

"Now Dashley and Tudor," continued Funnybird, "where's the grub you wouldn't give my brother?"

"Gone," replied Jack.

"I can see that; but where is it gone?"

Jack pointed to the region of his stomach, to convey the idea that he had eaten it.

"Eaten it?"

"Yes, haven't we come to Ea-ton?"

"I'll teach you to tell lies and make bad puns," said Funnybird; "we don't allow new boys to be too fresh."

He seized Jack by the arm, and twisting it half round, hit him with his fist on the muscular portion of it, causing him considerable pain.

Timor produced a knotted rope from his pocket, which he called his knout, and began, with Funnybird's help, to hit Owen on the back with it.

While this was going on Funnybird Minor hunted about like a cat for the good things which had been so carefully stowed away.

"I've got 'em," he cried, hauling the fowl and ham and tongue down from the top of the bed.

"All right. Take them away. They are confiscated," replied his brother.

Laughing merrily, Funnybird Minor was about to obey the welcome order, when a handsome fair young man about seventeen appeared on the threshold.

He had been attracted by the noise made by Jack and Owen, for it may be readily supposed that they did not maintain silence while they were being licked by two stronger and older boys than themselves, helped too by a third.

"Funnybird and Timor!" he exclaimed, "stop that. And you,"—he added to the other—"put those things back on the table. You ought to be ashamed of yourself to bag a fellow's grub, and especially a new fellow."

Funnybird Minor looked abashed, and did as he was told with an ill-grace, while his brother and Timor released their victims.

The newcomer was a fifth-form boy named Sutherland.

He was a thorough gentleman in every sense of the word.

An excellent scholar, he at the same time was a good cricketer—had been two years in the eleven, and excelled in boating.

His moral influence in the house was great, and because the boys knew that he could support it by physical force if he liked, they paid great respect to him.

"Can't you let a new fellow alone?" continued Sutherland. "The house is getting quite a bad name for bullying, and you two men are the principal cause of it."

"They cheeked my minor and shied bread at him," replied Funnybird, sulkily.

"Just leave them alone and clear out of here as soon as possible."

"I don't see what right you have to order us about."

"If you don't do as I tell you I'll call the captain of the house," said Sutherland.

It happened that Careless, the captain in question, came by at the time, and hearing Sutherland's voice, entered the room.

"I was looking for you!" he exclaimed. "The sixth and fifth forms are going to choose their fags for the half. But what's the row?"

"Oh, the old thing—Funnybird and Timor bullying as usual," replied Sutherland.

Careless was a good-natured boy, and he seldom interfered unless it was absolutely necessary.

In the present instance he thought that it was.

"You'll have to stop this, you fellows," he cried. "Two boys left our house last half and have gone to another because they were bullied so. They would not say who did it, but when my tutor spoke to me to-day about it I could have told him."

"Sneaks don't flourish at Eton," answered Funnybird.

"No," said Timor, "the atmosphere does not seem to agree with them."

"I don't know that a sneak is any worse than a bully," remarked Careless. "But this I do know, the house is getting a bad name, and Mr. Dryasdust has asked me as captain to stop it."

"Has he? Why doesn't he make you a private detective at once? I expect your father was one," laughed Funnybird Major.

This observation irritated Careless, who extended his hand and gave the speaker a box on the ear which sent him spinning, and caused his brother to get out of the door as quick as possible, abandoning all ulterior designs on the fowls and ham.

"What did you do that for?" asked Funnybird, clenching his fists.

"To teach you a lesson. Let these two new fellows alone. The same remark applies to you, Timor."

Funnybird and Timor walked out of the room with deep passion in their hearts, and Jack Dashley and Owen Tudor felt much relieved.

"If those men bully you any more come to me; my room is at the end of the passage!" exclaimed Careless. "I'm captain of this house, and by Jove! I'll take a little more trouble than I have hitherto done to preserve order. Come on, Sutherland, let us arrange about the fags."

"Shall we have to fag?" asked Jack.

"Yes; all boys not in the fifth form have to."

"I'd like to fag for you then, if I can," replied Jack.

"I can't promise you that," said Careless. "Because we put all the names in a bag, and the masters who are entitled to have fags draw for them."

"Will Funnybird and Timor draw?"

"Yes, they are entitled to one each."

"It will be a nice look out if they draw us. What shall we have to do?"

Careless smiled.

"Oh, nothing very bad," he replied. "Sutherland and I have been through it, and you see we are still alive. Don't meet trouble half-way; a good deal depends upon the master you get."

So saying, the captain of the house and Sutherland went away to arrange about the fags, and Jack and Owen sat down to finish their tea.

"We got out of that pretty well," remarked Owen, "though I feel sore from that Russian knout yet."

"They will let us alone after what Careless said, I should think," Jack observed.

A peculiar noise came from the adjoining room.

It was like one goat calling to another on the mountain top.

"Ba-a-a! Ba-a-a!"

"Hang it all!" exclaimed Owen, "that's Funnybird Minor. He's at it again. I'll goat him."

He jumped up and ran angrily into Funnybird's room, where he beheld that comic young gentleman leaning his head against the wall, engaged in the interesting occupation of "ba-ing," while seated in the arm-chair with which he had garnished his apartment was a short stout boy with a fat face, who was laughing till his sides ached.

This was Bill Bragg, a vulgar boy, who told no end of stories, and was always boasting of the "swells" he knew and the wonderful things he did, and the position of his friends at home.

The truth being that his father was a drysalter in the Barbican, who had married his cook, and having made a little money sent his son to a public school, choosing Eton as the most aristocratic.

There was nothing in all this for Bill Bragg to be ashamed of, but he always wanted to make himself out better than he really was, and this occasionally made him ridiculous, for he could not help being found out at times.

"Ba-a-a! m-a-a," went Funnybird Minor.

"Go it—what a lark!" exclaimed Bill Bragg, adding—as he saw Owen Tudor enter—"Oh, crikey! here's a case of scissors. The goat's come."

Jack followed Owen, because he felt bound to help him.

Without waiting to ask for any explanation, Owen gave Funnybird a kick which lifted him about three inches in the air, and landed him on all fours on the floor.

"Great Cæsar," cried Funnybird, "what's that?" It seemed as if the side of a house had fallen on me."

"It's only me," answered Owen. "I'm here if you want any more."

"I'm not a hog," replied Funnybird, rubbing his leg; "that will last me for to-night."

"Don't you imitate goats," said Owen. "If there are goats in Wales, they are better than English curs like you."

"I'll tell my brother," said Funnybird.

"If you do, I'll go to the captain of the house; he promised to protect us," exclaimed Jack Dashley.

"Us?" repeated Funnybird. "What have you to do with it?"

"We are chums. I've palled up with Tudor, and any one who offends him offends me. That's what's the matter."

Funnybird indulged in a sneer.

"I suppose you are some private school lad," he replied. "They are always fond of sneaking, but we'll quickly knock that out of you."

"I have been to a private school," answered Jack. "This is my first appearance at a public one, but I'm happy to say that we had no such fellow as you. If you talk about telling your brother, is not that as bad as my telling Careless?"

"All I know is, I'll have my revenge," growled Funnybird.

Seeing that he would not fight, and that he had no further inclination to ba-a, Owen was satisfied with the chastisement he had inflicted.

Bill Bragg was a great talker, and he could not resist the temptation to say something.

"That wasn't half a bad kick," he remarked. "I like to see everything slap-bang and all alive. The other day I kicked a crossing-sweeper right across the street for asking me for a penny."

"More shame for you," replied Jack.

"Oh, that's nothing. A week ago a fellow came playing an organ outside our house; he would'nt go away, so I gave him a sender which knocked him slick into his organ, slap-bang, and no mistake."

"What did he do then?"

"Crawled out again on the other side, and the music went on the same as ever, only a little out of tune."

Jack laughed, and was about to make some answer, when Timor entered the room.

"Where's Dashley," he asked.

"Here," replied Jack.

"You're my fag for this half," he continued, "and if you don't come up to time, I pity you, that's all."

Dashley felt as if some one had stabbed him with a knife.

Of all the fifth-form boys at Eton, Timor was the last he would have liked to fag for.

"I mess with Funnybird Major," said Timor; "and you will have to come at nine o'clock and get our breakfast ready. If the kettle doesn't boil and you spoil the tea in making it, I'm sorry for you, Where's Tudor?"

"I'm Tudor!" answered Owen.

"Oh, yes. I remember you," exclaimed Timor; "you are the man whose bird I gave freedom to. Well, you are Funnybird Major's fag, so both of you will have to wait on us."

Having made this announcement, the Russian went away, satisfied that he had caused the two boys as much discomfort as was possible in about the space of three minutes.

"My eyes!" said Bill Bragg, "won't you have a lively time of it? I fagged last half for Timor, and he's a beauty. On the fifth of November he put a torpedo on a chair, made me sit on it, lighted it, and sent me flying up to the ceiling, slap-bang, and all alive."

"Did it hurt you?" asked Jack.

"I couldn't wear a collar for a week. I stuck in the ceiling, and they had to make a hole in the roof to get me out, slap-bang, and all alive."

This was more than either Jack or Owen could stand, and they went back to their own rooms.

Jack helped Owen to make his room comfortable and put his things away, and then Owen performed the same kind offices for him, after which they sat by the fire, talking until supper time.

They were very much annoyed at the idea of having to fag for Timor and Funnybird, but as it was their luck to be drawn by them there was no help for it.

After supper and prayers, at which they saw quite a small army of boys, they went upstairs again.

Most of the fellows in their house had returned on the first day, though some of the fifth and sixth form claimed the privilege of the extra day accorded to them.

Feeling tired, they were not sorry to go to bed.

Susan came to take their candles.

Owen was sitting on Jack's bed in his nightshirt, and ran into his room.

"I think you'd better look out, sir!" she exclaimed.

"What for?" asked Jack.

"A new boy generally has some tricks played on him, and I heard Mr. Funnybird mention your name."

"I wish Funnybird would let me alone!" exclaimed Jack.

"He'll have to leave the house if he goes on the way he's been a-going, sir," replied Susan; "and Mr. Timor's worse than him. I'd lock my door, sir."

"There's no lock to it, Susan; I looked at it just now."

"Bless me! that's a fact. Well, you must get a bolt put on to-morrow; most gentlemen do. Good night, sir, and I hope as how you'll sleep well."

Jack thanked her, but he did not feel at his ease.

And though he courted sleep, it did not come.

He was thinking of Funnybird Major and Timor, wondering what they would do, and feeling in confusion about this new world of Eton, on the waters of which his frail barque had been launched.

While he half dozed he thought he heard footsteps approaching his room.

He listened.

It was not a mistake.

Some one was in the corridor.

His door opened.

He scarcely dared to breathe.

He heard, or rather felt, that some one was in the room.

What should he do?

His first impulse was to jump out of bed and ask what the intruder wanted, but resisting this, he remained perfectly still.

All at once he felt his feet going up in the air, and the blood rushed to his head.

Jack could not make out what was happening to him, but in less than ten seconds he was standing on his head, as it were.

There was a sharp click as the button was turned outside the bed, and he knew that he was "shut up."

Of all the practical jokes which an Etonian has to undergo, being shut up in a folding-bedstead is the worst.

Jack Dashley was unable to move.

He could not regain his erect position.

All he was able to accomplish was to keep the clothes from his mouth with his hands, and so get a little air.

He felt a sense of heaviness and approaching suffocation.

If this confinement lasted much longer he would die, for he was sure he could not bear it.

Oh, Heaven! what would he not have given for just one little breath of air!

He struggled like a maniac; his eyes seemed to be bursting out of his head, and he screamed hoarsely for help.

The bedclothes muffled his voice, and his piteous entreaties could not be heard.

"Help, help!" he cried, in a stifled voice.

But no help came.

He gave himself up for lost, and thinking of his mother, he tried to breathe a prayer, after which he grew dizzy, seeing green fields and hearing the notes of singing birds like a drowning man.

Suddenly he felt the bed pulled down.

The blood rushed from his head and began to circulate in his body once more.

A flood of cold air refreshed him.

He saw a light, and standing by his side was Sutherland.

"Are you better?" asked the latter, kindly.

Jack, after a time, gasped out—

"Yes, thank you."

"I suspected something of this kind," continued Sutherland, "and that is what made me come to your room."

"You came just in time. I thought I was dying," cried Jack, still lying helpless on the bed.

"It is no joke to be shut up. I have gone through it myself, though, thank goodness, I was never cowardly enough to do it to anyone else. These infernal bullies ought to be punished."

"Who did it, do you think?" asked Jack, sitting up at last.

"Oh, Timor and Funnybird. I saw them in the passage, but they ran away when they twigged me."

Jack got out of bed and shook himself.

"I'm all right now," he exclaimed. "But, I say, have you been to look after Tudor?"

"Not yet."

"If they would attack me, you may depend they would go for him too; my chum, I mean. Perhaps he is as badly off as I was."

"That is so," said Sutherland. "We will see. Come with me."

They hastily made their way into the next room, and with the aid of Sutherland's candle, looked for Owen.

The bed was rumpled, and had evidently been slept in, but they could find no trace of its owner.

"Why, where on earth is he?" said Jack Dashley.

Sutherland looked around in a perplexed manner.

"They cannot have killed him, and thrown him out of the window," continued Jack.

This remark gave Sutherland an idea, for he went to the window, which was open, and looked out.

"Here he is," he cried, beginning to haul up something.

Jack hastened to his side, and saw the two ends of a sheet tied to the bar which ran across the centre of the window.

Owen Tudor had been placed in the sheet, and lowered from the window, being left to hang in mid-air until his tormentors chose to release him.

If he had struggled in the least degree, he would have dropped out, and falling on the ground below, seriously injured himself.

He was naturally very much alarmed, and felt as much relieved as Jack did when he was released.

"Are you hurt, Owen?" asked Jack, squeezing his hand.

"Not much," replied Tudor. "The beasts seized me when I was half asleep, and nearly strangled me, so that I shouldn't holloa. They then put me in the sheet and slung me out of the window, telling me if I struggled I should be killed."

"How long have you been there?"

"Oh, a good five minutes, though it seemed an age. I daren't move. If this is coming to Eton, I wish I had stayed at home."

"It doesn't always happen," said Sutherland. "Those bullies are a disgrace to the house."

"And we have to fag for them," groaned Owen.

"Never mind," replied Sutherland. "You have a friend in me, and they are afraid of Careless. If they perform on you again, let us know. Now go to bed. I don't think you will be troubled again to-night."

He left them, and after condoling with one another, they retired to rest a second time, Sutherland being right in his conjecture, for they were not disturbed any more that night.

CHAPTER III.

IN WINDSOR FOREST.

PUNCTUALLY at seven Susan called the boys, and turning out of bed, they dressed, feeling that strange sense of loneliness which one always experiences at waking up in a strange place.

They soon found their way to the

school-yard, where all the schoolrooms were, by following the crowd of boys hastening from the different houses, and took their places in the Upper School with the rest of their division.

As it was their first morning, and they were not supplied with books yet, they were not called upon to do any work.

After school they went back to their tutor's for prayers, and then proceeded to Timor's room to do their fagging.

It was very handsomely furnished, for he had the command of money, and had not spared any expense.

The walls were covered with handsome engravings.

He had flowers in his window, and being fond of music, had bought a piano.

Jack went to the cupboard and took out the tea, while Owen saw that the kettle boiled, and Timor and Funnybird talked together near the window.

"How many spoonfuls of tea shall I put in ? " asked Jack.

"Find out," replied Funnybird. "You two mess together, and you ought to know how much is required for two."

"Do you like it strong ? "

"Yes. Don't bother me."

Jack made the tea, placed the teapot on the table, and was about to walk away.

"Where are you off to ? " asked Timor.

"To my own room. Don't you suppose I want some breakfast ? " replied Jack.

"Well, you won't have any yet. Take this shilling and go down to Webber's for a shilling's worth of hot sausages."

"And you, Tudor," said Funnybird Major, "cut along to the baker and bring a couple of hot college rolls."

He gave him some money, and the fags departed to get their hats.

In the passage they met Bill Bragg.

"Were are you off to ? " he asked.

"Sausages," replied Jack in a melancholy tone of voice.

"Hot college rolls," answered Owen, in an equally lachrymose manner, " and I don't know where the bakery is."

"And I could not tell Webber's from Kamschatka," said Jack.

"I fag for Careless," exclaimed Bragg. I'm going for rolls, so one of you can come with me. Webber's is down by

Barn's Pool. My master looked as if he would like to have sausages this morning, but he didn't send me."

"Why didn't he ? " asked Jack.

"Because he looked in my eye and saw an expression there, slap-bang and all alive, that told him I wouldn't go. If Careless said a word to me I didn't like, I'd back out of the room and let him do his own fagging."

Unfortunately for the boaster, Careless had been into some one's room to borrow a Greek Lexicon, and he heard this remark of his fag's.

"Oh, you would, eh ? " he exclaimed. " We will see. When you have brought me my hot rolls you shall go up to Layton's and fetch me a penny bun. Cut along."

Bill Bragg looked very foolish, as well he might, for Layton's was a confectioner's shop in Windsor, nearly opposite the Curfew Tower of the Castle.

If he ran all the way there and back it would take him half-an-hour to go, and he would have no time to eat his own breakfast.

He might have bought such a simple thing as a bun anywhere, but he knew that his master would look at the bag, and if he did not see Layton's name on it he would be sent back.

"Shall you go ? " asked Jack.

"Yes, I'll humour him this time. He looks as if he wanted a bun, and he is not a bad sort when you come to know him. This is the second half I have fagged for him."

"Indeed."

"The fact is I begin quite to like him."

"So I should think."

"And I can't find it in my heart to refuse him anything," said Bragg. " Ta-ta! stroll on. I mustn't keep him waiting, poor fellow."

He and Owen started off to the bakery, and Jack went after the sausages, laughing at the ingenious way in which Bragg got himself out of a dilemma.

When fagging was over he and Owen had their breakfast, and came to the conclusion that though it was a nuisance, there was not anything very difficult after all in the system.

At eleven they had to go into school and translate some easy Latin, such as Cæsar or Livy.

Then the time until dinner, from a quarter to twelve to two, was their own.

Jack Dashley had heard so much about Windsor Castle that he was very anxious to visit and roam in the park or forest.

He thought of the dungeons, vaults, sliding panels in the old towers, and the subterranean passages that must exist.

He called to mind the legend of Herne the Hunter, and wondered whether the weird huntsman and his coal-black steed were ever seen now.

Owen readily agreed to walk up town with him, and they only regretted that they had no companion to show them the way.

They were standing in the schoolyard near the statue, gazing at the size of the old chapel.

On the other side was Lower School and Long Chamber, in which were to be seen the collegians in their long gowns.

Suddenly Jack saw Bragg running towards them.

"I say!" he cried; "your fools if you stop here."

"Why are we?"

"You see those fives courts alongside the chapel? Well, they will be filled soon with fellows playing fives, and they always look round for a lower boy to fag for them. It means picking up balls for a couple of hours, that's all. Oh, I'm slap-bang, and all alive."

They all hastened to avoid a species of fagging which was anything but agreeable.

"Are you going to be a wet bob or a dry bob?" asked Bragg. "Every one here has to be one or the other. Let me explain: a wet bob means a boating man; a dry bob, a cricketer."

"I don't know yet," replied Jack; "though I think I prefer the water."

"Where are you going now?" asked Bragg, who was not backward at asking questions.

"Up to see the Castle? Will you come with us?"

"Just to oblige you," answered Bragg; "though I don't care much about it; you see, I go there so often. My people are very intimate at court, and the Queen invites me up to play with the princes until it becomes a bore."

"Then you know the Queen?"

"Oh, yes, slap-bang and all alive. I call her Vic, and I'm never anything else than Billy."

Jack could not refrain from smiling at the impudence of the fellow's stories, in which he knew there was not a grain of truth, but as he found him a little amusing, he did not say anything.

They walked up the Eton High Street and into Windsor, where the castle burst upon them in all its beauty and grandeur.

Ascending by the hundred steps at the base of the Curfew Tower, they reached the terrace, on which they walked, afterwards skirting the Round Tower, from the top of which floated the Royal Standard, which indicated that Her Majesty was at home.

"Vic's in," said Bragg, carelessly. "But I don't think I'll call on her to-day. Let's get into the park. We may see Herne the Hunter."

A thrill of superstitious fear ran through the veins of Jack and Owen at the mention of the name.

"Do you believe in him?" Jack asked.

"Why shouldn't I, when I saw him one day on his coal-black horse, breathing fire and smoke? Slap-bang and all alive."

"What did you do—run?"

"Not I," replied Bragg; "I chucked a stone and it went clean through him; nothing but a spirit, my boy."

They quitted the castle by the postern at the top of the hill, and got into the forest at the beginning of the Long Walk.

The season being mild and forward, the trees were just beginning to bud, the grass looked fresh and green, the sun shone brightly, the birds sang blithely, and the merry brown hares sat in the ferns, while the rooks cawed overhead as they built their nests.

Cutting across an open glade, they came to a lot of fern, in which some deer were grazing.

"Look out, young gentlemen," cried a man, appearing from behind a tree.

He was dressed in a coat of Lincoln green and corduroy trousers; in his hand he carried a gun,

"That's Gunstock the keeper," said Bragg; "I know him."

"It seems to me you know everybody," answered Jack.

www.ingramcontent.com/pod-product-compliance
Lightning Source LLC
Chambersburg PA
CBHW080842250626

47161CB00009B/3157